Sleep Out

Sleep Out

Carol and Donald Carrick

CLARION BOOKS

NEW YORK

Clarion Books, a Houghton Mifflin Company imprint
215 Park Avenue South, New York, NY 10003
Copyright © 1973 by Carol and Donald Carrick, ISBN: 0-395-28780-4.
Paperback ISBN: 0-89919-083-9
Library of Congress Catalog Card Number: 72-88539.
HOR 20 19 18 17 16 15 14 13

Christopher got a sleeping bag for his birthday. A sleeping bag, a canteen for water, and a flashlight.

"It's for the country," his father said. "We'll sleep out next weekend when we go to the cottage for the summer."

"Oh," Christopher complained. "That's too long to wait."

He dragged all the gear downstairs to the back yard to try it out.

Sparrows flew from the bird bath to the tree. In its shade, where it would seem more like night, Christopher opened the sleeping bag.

He got inside and scrunched up his eyes. A heavy truck rumbled by in the street out front. Then he heard the Post Office helicopter and looked for it through the treetop.

His dog, Bodger, was patiently watching him. When he saw Christopher's eyes open, he came over and licked his face.

The lady next door rattled her window open and began pulling in the wash. She smiled at Christopher. "You playing nice?" she asked.

She really spoiled the whole thing. He couldn't pretend to be all by himself in the woods when nosy people interrupted.

On Saturday morning they loaded the car and got ready to leave. It was a long trip to the country. Christopher and Bodger piled into the back seat with the suitcases and sleeping bag.

Christopher was full of exciting plans for sleeping out that night. He was going to be a scout for the army. Or maybe he would be an Indian. . . .

"I'm going to camp near the brook, where I can fill my canteen."

"Your father's too tired to camp out tonight," said his mother over her shoulder. "And there are too many things to do before we're settled."

"I'll go out myself, then," answered Christopher.

"You better wait till your father can take you."

"I'd rather go by myself."

"It's all right." His father smiled. "I'll help Christopher pack. He's picked a good spot and he can always come back if he changes his mind."

But Christopher was certain. "I won't change my mind."

While his mother and father unloaded the car, Christopher collected his sleeping bag, canteen, pillow, a book about Indians, and a compass. It made a big pile on the front porch of the cottage. His father helped him roll everything into a neat bundle and his mother gave him food to take along.

"I'll see you tomorrow," Christopher said as he started off.

Up on the road Bodger barked, answering the faint call of someone else's dog on another farm. He tried to come along but Christopher told him to go back home.

As he took a short cut through the pasture, Christopher could see the white woolly backs of the sheep in the moonlight and hear the leader's tinkling bell.

Christopher found his camping place in a stand of pine trees. He unrolled the pack on a thick growth of moss and ate his sandwich and cookies.

There was cold chocolate milk. When he finished it he rinsed the canteen in the brook, and refilled it with cold water. Insects danced in the rays of the flashlight and brushed his face.

He crawled into the sleeping bag and lay watching the wink of fireflies. Two trees rubbed together and startled him. A mosquito whined in his ear.

Christopher wriggled down inside where it felt dark and safe. He tried telling himself stories. His mother had read a book to him about cowboys and how they slept out under the stars. Sometimes a snake crawled into their bedroll to get warm. Christopher got quickly out of his bag.

"Being by yourself isn't very much fun," he thought.

The tops of the taller trees began to rock, and rain suddenly rattled on the leaves.

At first the trees kept Christopher dry. But as the branches drooped, heavy with water, the drops trickled through. He got back inside his sleeping bag and zipped it shut over his head. He couldn't breathe. It was too hot and stuffy in there. Maybe he could find a better place till the rain stopped.

Low branches slapped Christopher's face as he left the pine grove. His sleeping bag wasn't rolled up so neatly this time and it caught on the bushes.

He decided it would be easier walking down the road. His
pack was getting heavy and he started to drag it.

There was a crashing in the weeds and a dark shape broke
out onto the road. Christopher grabbed the flashlight from his
belt and turned it on the thing. An old fat porcupine waddled
away from him.

Then he heard the howl. "A wolf!" thought Christopher.
And it was between him and home.

Up the road a little was an empty farmhouse. Christopher ran as fast as he could toward it. The sleeping bag bumped his legs, and the canteen and flashlight on his belt made a terrible clatter. "The noise will give me away," he said to himself. "Wolves have sharp ears."

Long ago someone had broken the lock on the door of the farmhouse. Christopher had been inside lots of times with his friends. He thought it would be safest upstairs.

The moon was out again and shining into the room. Christopher felt better sitting in one of the darker corners. He tried to make no sounds, but it was hard to stay still. Mice were scratching in the wall behind him. How long would he have to wait before it was all right to leave?

The front door creaked. Big paws clattered up the stairs. The wolf had smelled Christopher's trail right to his hiding place. He heard loud panting in the hall and the click of nails on the bare boards.

Christopher looked desperately for a hiding place in the empty room. He saw only a clothes closet without a door. There was a lot of snuffling outside. He ran into the closet and pulled the curtain in front of him. The old latch rattled until the bedroom door was pushed open.

Then the wolf rushed in, leaped on Christopher happily, and licked his face. It was Bodger, so pleased with himself for tracking Christopher down.

By now it was late and Christopher was too tired to carry the pack any more. With big warm Bodger there the night didn't seem frightening.

Christopher unrolled his sleeping bag and crawled in. Bodger lay down with a thump and a sigh.

The morning sun turned the dark room from black to gray and the fog lifted above the trees where the birds were noisily singing. Christopher's eyes opened with surprise. Then he smiled as he realized he had slept out all night by himself.

As he carefully rolled up his pack, he felt a little stiff and a little tired, but mostly he was very, very hungry. Bodger jumped to his feet and shook himself.

When Christopher reached home, he saw his father putting up the screen door.

"Well, you really did it," his father said. "You slept out by yourself. How was it?"

"It was really great, except I got a little scared. It started to rain and I went to the farm house and Bodger found me and we slept there together. But it would have been more fun if you had come along."

"How about tonight?" his father asked. "We can set up the tent."

"Oh, boy!" Christopher said, running inside for some breakfast. "Hey, Mom! Guess what? Dad and I are going to sleep out tonight."